FROM THE FILMS OF

Harry Potter

DESTROY THE HORCRUXES

WIZARDING WORLD

SCHOLASTIC INC.

ISBN 978-1-338-76763-6

10 9 8 7 6 5 4 3 2 1   21 22 23 24 25
Printed in China 62

First edition 2021

By Terrance Crawford
Book design by Jessica Meltzer and Jessica Dacher

DARK MAGIC has long ravished the

wizarding world. But perhaps no evil can come close to Lord Voldemort (formerly known as Tom Riddle), who wielded enough Dark magic to split his soul not once, but *seven* times. Each time he did so, Voldemort left behind a piece of himself secured in an object that was important to him, like his childhood diary and his family's ancestral ring.

These items are called Horcruxes. As Professor Horace Slughorn told young Tom, "a Horcrux is an object in which a person has concealed part of their soul." So long as the Horcrux remains intact, that person cannot die.

HORCRUXES are potent objects that can only be destroyed by powerful magic.

Destroying a Horcrux is, of course, no easy feat. It requires a method of destruction that damages the Horcrux beyond repair.

Basilisk venom, an extremely poisonous substance, is the first medium with which we see Harry destroy a Horcrux. He uses it on Tom Riddle's diary in the Chamber of Secrets. Throughout the films, we also see Neville Longbottom, Ron Weasley, Albus Dumbledore, Hermione Granger, and even— accidentally—Draco Malfoy's cohort Gregory Goyle help destroy Horcruxes.

In this book, imagine you will be destroying Horcruxes. Use your pens, kitchen sink, fingers, and more to shred this very book—just as we see Harry employ magic to end Voldemort.

Harry:
But if you could
find them all, if you did
destroy each Horcrux—

Dumbledore:
One DESTROYS
Voldemort.

—Harry Potter and the
Half-Blood Prince

Smear
ink
on this
page.

Drip
WATER
on this
page.

AGUAMENTI!

USE A PEN TO SCRATCH OUT EVERY WORD ON THESE PAGES.

SECTUMSEMPRA!

BORGIN AND BURKES

HAND OF GLORY

CRUCIATUS CURSE

BASILISK

DEMENTORS

SEVERING CHARM

DEATH EATER

Unforgivable Curses

HEX

PETRIFICATION

CRUCIO!

Imperius Curse

BOGGART

ACROMANTULA

AVADA KEDAVRA!

VAMPIRE

OPAL NECKLACE

SPIRIT

BANSHEE

IMPERIO!

Hag

GRINDYLOW

ZOMBIE

WEREWOLF

Jinx

DROP THIS BOOK FROM A GREAT HEIGHT

WINGARDIUM LEVIOSA!

Soil
this
page
with
DIRT.

Let an **ICE CUBE** *melt* on this page.

PRESS A
FLOWER OR LEAF
ONTO THIS PAGE.

BRIGHTLY COLOR THIS PAGE.

LUMOS

DARKEN THIS ENTIRE PAGE.

TAKE A *deep* BREATH
AND LEAVE THIS PAGE BLANK.

LEAVE THIS
BOOK UNDER
SOMETHING
HEAVY.

TEAR OUT THIS PAGE,

RIP IT UP,

THEN PIECE IT
BACK TOGETHER.

Write the same word
OVER and OVER and
OVER and OVER &
OVER.

REMOVE
THIS PAGE
ENTIRELY.

WRITE A STORY ABOUT SOMETHING THAT HAPPENED TO YOU, THEN ~~SCRATCH~~ IT OUT.

_____
_____
_____
_____
_____
_____
_____
_____
_____
_____

OBLIVIATE!

_____
_____
_____
_____
_____
_____
_____
_____

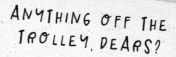

ANYTHING OFF THE TROLLEY, DEARS?

— TROLLEY WITCH,
HARRY POTTER AND THE SORCERER'S STONE

CRUSH

SOMETHING DELICIOUS AGAINST THIS PAGE.

PUNCH STARS
OUT OF THESE PAGES
AND LOOK THROUGH THE HOLES
AT THE NIGHT SKY.

It's not real, the ceiling.
It's just bewitched to look
like the night sky . . .
— Hermione Granger,
Harry Potter and the Sorcerer's Stone

IF YOU CAN READ
THIS,YOU DIDN'T MAKE
ENOUGH STARS.

GO BACK AND TRY AGAIN.

Color this **WHOLE** page yellow.

Now . . . When I call your name, you will come forth. I shall place the Sorting Hat on your head, and you will be sorted into your houses.

—Minerva McGonagall, *Harry Potter and the Sorcerer's Stone*

Decorate this page with your house colors.

- SLYTHERIN
- HUFFLEPUFF
- RAVENCLAW
- GRYFFINDOR

Poke several holes on the bottom of this page.

HOGWARTS TERMS ALWAYS BEGIN WITH A FEAST IN THE GREAT HALL.

MASH PART OF YOUR DINNER AGAINST THIS PAGE.

Eye of rabbit, harp-string hum, turn this water into rum!

— Seamus Finnigan, *Harry Potter and the Sorcerer's Stone*

DRAW SMOKE.

RUB THIS PAGE WITH A COIN UNTIL IT TEARS.

DRAW YOUR
NAME IN
BUBBLE
LETTERS.

TEAR
THIS PAGE
OUT AND
TAPE IT
ELSEWHERE
IN THE
BOOK.

WINGARDIUM LEVIOSA!

It's Leviosa, not leviosAAA . . .
—Hermione Granger, *Harry Potter and the Sorcerer's Stone*

Throw this book across the room
(but not at anyone or anything breakable, please).

DOG-EAR THIS PAGE.

Use this page
as a coaster for
lukewarm tea.

COVER THIS PAGE WITH WRAPPING PAPER.

Rip a few bristles out of your kitchen broomstick and tape them here.

MATCH RON'S SWEATER BY COVERING THIS
PAGE WITH A DRAWING OF THE LETTER R.

Create your own
Weasley sweater
by gluing different
textures to this
page.

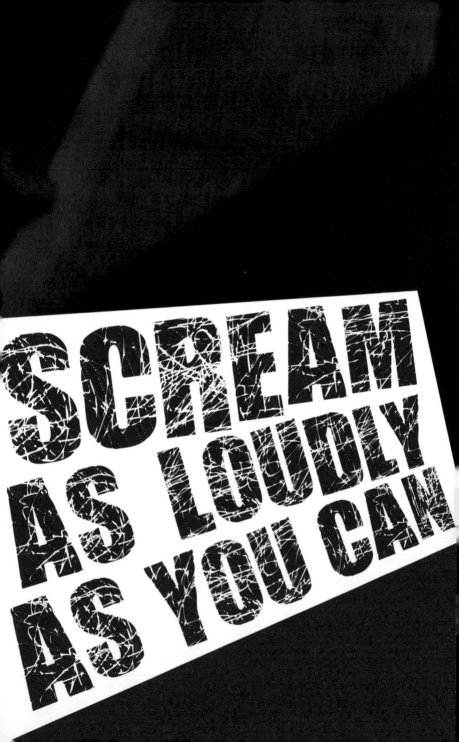

INTO THE SPACE BETWEEN THESE TWO PAGES

GO OUTSIDE. Cover this page with pebbles, grass, and whatever else you may find.

Brew some tea.
Rub the tea bag
or leaves on
this page.

HARRY LEARNS THAT THE MIRROR OF ERISED SHOWS NOT OUR REFLECTIONS, BUT OUR HEARTS' DESIRES. DO WHATEVER YOUR HEART DESIRES WITH THIS PAGE.

WRITE OR DRAW ON THIS PAGE BACKWARD.

CRINKLE THIS PAGE.

PETRIFICUS TOTALUS!

THEN FLATTEN IT AS BEST YOU CAN.

< · < · < · > · > · > · >

FLOREAN
FORTESCUE'S
ICE CREAM
PARLOR
TODAY'S

SHINE A FLASHLIGHT AT THIS PAGE.

WITH **BOTH** EYES CLOSED, DRAW A LIGHTNING **BOLT** ON THIS PAGE.

CUT A HOLE into this page.

Cover this page with Spellotape,

OR your nearest non-magical

equivalent.

Fill this page with pictures of people who you love.

FILL THIS PAGE WITH PICTURES OF YOUR CELEBRITY CRUSH.

DRAW A
MANDRAKE
ON THIS
PAGE.

Get your hands dirty,
then wipe them across this page.

SCRAPE THIS BOOK ACROSS THE FLOOR.

THROW A BALL AT THIS BOOK.

USE THIS BOOK TO BAT OR SWAT SOMETHING AWAY.

Not bad.
You'd make
a fair Beater!
—Oliver Wood, *Harry Potter and the Sorcerer's Stone*

MAKE A MESS ON THIS PAGE.

Drag something SLIMY across this page.

WRITE something in a language only you can understand, even if you made it up.

WRITE A MESSAGE IN RED ON THIS PAGE.

BRACKIUM EMENDO!

CRACK this book's SPINE.

I can mend bones in a heartbeat, but growing them back?

—Poppy Pomfrey, *Harry Potter and the Chamber of Secrets*

 Did you know? A human adult's spine is comprised of twenty-six bones.

TAPE A PIECE OF HAIR TO THIS PAGE.

FLUXWEED

KNOTGRASS

LACEWING FLIES

LEECHES

POWDERED BICORN HORN

SHREDDED BOOMSLANG SKIN

OBLIVIATE!

Leave this page alone for now,
but remember it for later.

EXPELLIARMUS!

Expel this book from your grasp with force.

Together we shall cast ourselves into the future!

—Sybill Trelawney, *Harry Potter and the Prisoner of Azkaban*

TAKE THIS PAGE AND USE IT TO CLEAN THE SPILL ON THE NEXT PAGE.

GO TO YOUR KITCHEN.

CONCOCT A POTION,

LIST THE INGREDIENTS,

AND DRIP IT ACROSS THIS PAGE.

FILL THESE PAGES WITH
PICTURES OR DRAWINGS OF
ANIMALS.

**CUT AND PASTE
PICTURES FROM MAGAZINES
AND NEWSPAPERS HERE.**

Stick *feathers* to this page.

WRITE DOWN EVERY SPELL YOU CAN REMEMBER.

STUPEFY!

OPPUGNO!

ACCIO!

ALOHOMORA!

REDUCTO!

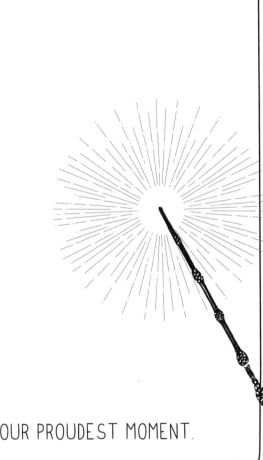

DRAW YOUR PROUDEST MOMENT.

COVER THIS PAGE WITH STAMPS.

PRIVET DRIVE

At Hogwarts, **SEVEN** is the most powerful number. Cover this page with the number **7**.

MAKE AN **IDENTICAL MESS** BY THINLY PAINTING THIS PAGE AND SHUTTING THE BOOK.

Ah, that's why it's so brilliant!
—Fred Weasley, *Harry Potter and the Goblet of Fire*

BECAUSE it's
so pathetically
dim-witted!

—George Weasley, Harry Potter
and the Goblet of Fire

WEASLEY&
WEASLEY&

Cover this page with candy wrappers!

EYEBALL BONANZA

FORTUNA MAJOR

SLASH THE PORTRAIT.

Cover this page with things that scare you.

COVER this page
with THINGS
that make you

LAUGH.

DRAW A MAP
TO SOMETHING

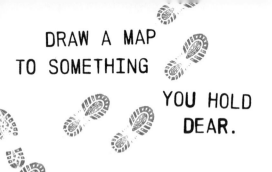

YOU HOLD
DEAR.

EXPECTO PATRONUM!

Fill this page with good thoughts.

Draw a **PAW** print on this page.

Pretend you're the
Whomping Willow.

THROW this
book around.

FOLD THE
TWO CORNERS
OF THIS PAGE INTO THE
CENTER AND LEAVE THEM THAT WAY.

Invite a friend OR family
member to draw on this page.

WRITE OR DRAW THE **SAME** EVENT
FROM TWO POINTS OF VIEW.

GO BACK TO THE BEGINNING AND
REDECORATE
THE COVER AND TITLE PAGE.

When in doubt, I find retracing my steps to be a wise place to begin. Good luck.

—Albus Dumbledore, *Harry Potter and the Prisoner of Azkaban*

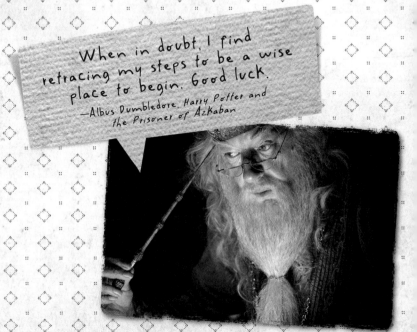

STICK THESE TWO PAGES TOGETHER.

EPOXIMISE!

Create art without lifting your hand.

MORSMORDRE!

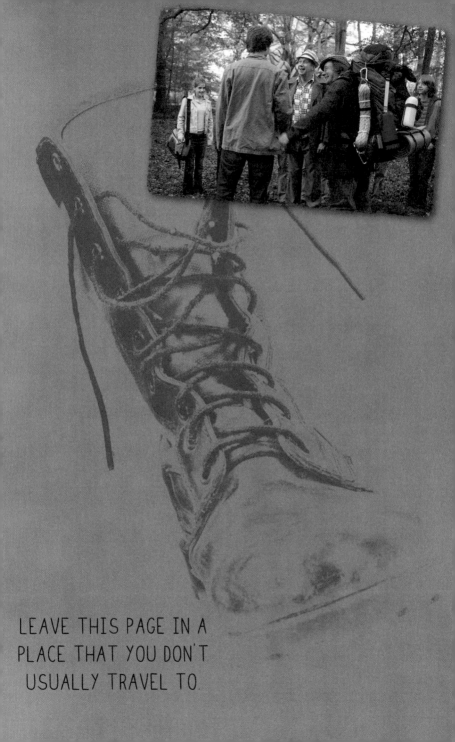

LEAVE THIS PAGE IN A
PLACE THAT YOU DON'T
USUALLY TRAVEL TO.

DRAW ON THIS PAGE WITH YOUR
EYES CLOSED.

Everyone dresses
in their finest robes for the Yule Ball.
Fancily decorate this page.

TEAR OUT AND ROLL THIS PAGE INTO A SCROLL.

Spill a drink on this page.

TAKE THIS BOOK IN THE BATH.

Write your own newspaper headline.

DOUSE THIS PAGE
WITH HAIR SPRAY OR GEL.

STAND UP

+

STRETCH.

Write a personal story.

Draw a maze.

Speedily
COLOR THIS PAGE GREEN.

KEDAVRA!

AVADA

DRAW WITH YOUR NONDOMINANT HAND.

Trace your arm on this page
and design your own symbol.

SCRUB this page with a sponge.

LEVICORPUS!

DRAW SOMETHING WHILE
EITHER YOU
OR THE BOOK IS
UPSIDE DOWN.

VERA VERTO!

TURN THIS PAGE INTO SOMETHING.

ROLL THIS PAGE INTO A FUNNEL AND **SHOUT** THROUGH IT. THEN ROLL IT BACK.

SONORUS!

TAPE OBJECTS TO
THIS PAGE TO FIND
LATER.

GET THIS PAGE *signed* BY AS MANY PEOPLE AS YOU CAN.

Hermione Granger

Harry Potter

Luna Lovegood

Ron Weasley

Neville Longbottom

Dumbledore's Army
D.A.

Ginny Weasley

REMOVE THIS PAGE AND MAKE IT AS small AS POSSIBLE.

CUT THIS PAGE INTO AS MANY PIECES AS POSSIBLE.

REDUCTO!

SECTUMSEMPRA!

MARK THIS PAGE WITH RECKLESS ABANDON.

RIP OUT THIS PAGE

AND PASTE IT IN ANOTHER

PART OF THE BOOK.

EPISKEY!

RIP THIS PAGE TO SHREDS,

THEN PIECE IT BACK TOGETHER.

SCRATCH YOUR NAME INTO THIS PAGE.

Spray this page with a fragrance.

The most powerful love potion in the world. It's rumored to smell differently to each person according to what attracts them.

—Hermione Granger, Harry Potter and the Half-Blood Prince

Put on lipstick and decorate
this page with kisses.

Mail this page to a friend.

OWL POST

USE THIS SPACE TO LIST THINGS THAT BOTHER YOU.

- _____
- _____
- _____
- _____
- _____
- _____
- _____
- _____
- _____

RUB THIS PAGE AGAINST GRASS.

DRAG THIS PAGE THROUGH THE

DUST.

☞ **YOU** EMANATE

and **CAUGHT** PRESS

PLEASE UNDER

INFORMATION

THE THE

SPELL FOR

she is a

CAUTION ARMY OF

REWARD *truth*

MAGIC

CURSE

appeared

CONCERNING

YOUR PERSON

ANY SIGHTED *lies* dark

TO

LEADING IMPERIO

CONSTANT VIGILANCE!

US sent EATERS

DEATH ZOMBIE

they VILLAGE MINISTRY

ARE AMONG

DRAW SOMETHING.

ON THE PREVIOUS PAGE, COVER WHAT YOU'VE JUST DRAWN.

HIDE A SECRET MESSAGE
SOMEWHERE IN THIS BOOK.
THEN WRITE A CLUE HERE.

Decorate this page with every color at your disposal.

DR**O**P TEARS ON THIS PAGE.

DRAW THE DEATHLY HALLOWS
SYMBOL ALL OVER THIS PAGE.

CREATE A COLLAGE USING THINGS YOU WOULD OTHERWISE THROW AWAY.

Decorate this
page *vibrantly*.

COVER THIS PAGE WITH SOMETHING STICKY.

Close this book and sit up TALL.

BURY THIS PAGE.

Properly . . .
Without magic.

—Harry Potter, *Harry Potter and the Deathly Hallows - Part 1*

Dobby never meant to kill! Dobby only meant to maim . . . or seriously injure!

—Dobby, *Harry Potter and the Deathly Hallows – Part 1*

DESTROY THIS PAGE IN A MANNER OF YOUR CHOOSING.

NOW THAT
YOU'RE A PRO
AT DESTROYING
THIS BOOK
AND THE
HORCRUXES
IN IT, PLACE IT
SOMEWHERE
NICE AND ON
DISPLAY.